Porky Pies

Wolves, Squeals and Dodgy Deals
A play with songs for school performances

Text, songs and illustrations by
Robin Kingsland

A & C BLACK • LONDON

Contents

A Letter from the Playwright

Porky Pies is a comic courtroom drama based on well-known nursery characters. Having spent a lot of time recently in a number of primary schools, I am well aware of the need for flexibility in plays written for children. So although *Porky Pies* can be performed as a musical show, with nursery rhyme interludes and musical numbers (sung to the music at the back of the book), it can also be a straight play with dramatic recitations of the various songs where they occur. For those schools who want to put on a single show, involving all the children from reception up, a reception 'choir' could sing the relevant nursery rhymes as they appear in the script when the characters come on. Alternatively, they could sing all the nursery rhymes as an overture. With fewer children to accommodate, the nursery rhyme tunes could simply be played as introductory themes, or ignored altogether.

Casting is another area where flexibility is important. Teachers often find that a lot of children hope to be in the play. Some want to act their socks off, some want to sing their hearts out, some want to dance up a storm, and some just want to raise the roof with laughter. And among all of those hearts and socks and storms and roof damage, there are some who want to be in, but not have too much to learn, and others who want to be on as much as possible thank you, but not say anything, and others who... well, you get the picture. I have also tried to bear in mind the following things when writing this play:

- Spreading the load of 'stage time', so that no child has too much responsibility
- Giving everybody their 'moment' on stage

- Simplicity of staging, sound effects and music
- Economy in costume and prop requirements
- Pitching the play so that children and adults will both enjoy it
- Oh, and making it a good funny story!

You will find a couple of references to popular TV – specifically 'Scooby Doo' and 'Mr Benn'. If these don't feel right, please feel free to cut them. On the other hand, if certain lines or circumstances in the play seem to suggest local areas, then do add references of your own. A play always goes better if it is linked to the locality. In particular, I draw your attention to the reference at the end of Bo Peep's song, *'The Only Ewe That I Adore'*. In this spoof Country and Western ballad, I have included a line saying that one sheep is still 'M.I.A.'. This is an army term for 'Missing In Action'. Although it's a bit obscure, I left it in because a) I think it's funny, and b) because it fits so well with the C & W style, and with my vision of Bo as a cross between a Dresden shepherdess and a southern belle. You could also use it to create a new local reference by including something or somewhere near the school that begins with the letter A. Then, when the line has been sung, the actress can stop and speak the following explanatory line. "That's missing in Acton/Accrington/Aston..." before continuing with the final line of the song. With any luck, it'll get a big laugh!

That's all from me. I have had tremendous fun writing this play and I can only hope you have as much fun producing it.

Good luck!
Robin Kingsland

Characters In Order Of Appearance

Bea Bear (a TV news reporter)
Dexter (Bea's cameraman)
The Lawyers: the Defence
                        the Prosecution
Tommy Thin (a tearaway)
The Courtroom Cleaner
The Clerk of the Court
The Court Policeman
Polly Flinders (a private detective)
John Muddlecombe (Polly's partner)
The Judge
The Wolves: Big Bad Wolf
                        Little Bad Wolf
                        Knuckles

The Pigs: Pig Iron
                        Pig Sty
                        Pig Malion
Bo Peep (a shepherdess)
Raglan (a sheep)
Mr Mary (a householder)
Mrs Mary (his wife)
Mary Mary (their daughter)
Eunice (a ewe)
Mother Hubbard (a shopkeeper)
Crowd Leader
Others: Members of the jury, including rabbits
            A flock of sheep
            Members of the Public Gallery in court
            A mob

List of Scenes and their Locations

The play is simply divided into two halves and the scenes are not numbered as such. However, these divisions might be useful for scheduling rehearsals.

Songs and Nursery Rhymes in the play
(See note in 'A Letter from the Playwright')

Part One

Outside the Woodland Courtroom. Enter BEA BEAR, News Reporter for WXTV News. She is clearly flustered. She checks her clothes, brushes down her hair.

BEA: Right. Got everything? Microphone – check. Notes – check. Lucky paperclip... lucky paperclip... *(She finally finds it.)* Phew! – Check. Right... *(in presenter-mode)* Hello. Bea Bear here, reporting for WXTV from the Woodland Courtroom where... where... Where is my cameraman? Dexter?

(Enter DEXTER with a movie camera.)

BEA: Dexter! At last. What kept you? Never mind! Don't talk. Just get that camera running.

DEXTER: All right. Keep your hair on. Relax!

BEA: Stop telling me to relax! I am relaxed. Can't you see how relaxed I am?

(She strokes her lucky paperclip to calm herself.)

DEXTER: What's that?

BEA: This? Nothing. Just my lucky paperclip.

DEXTER: A lucky paperclip?!

BEA: This paperclip has been with me since my first day in Television. As long as I have this, I know nothing can go wrong!

(BEA turns on her heel... and walks straight into the DEFENCE LAWYER as he enters. Papers go everywhere.)

BEA: I'm terribly sorry!

DEFENCE : *(flustered)* Oh dear... Oh deary, dear!

DEXTER: *(aside)* Why wasn't I running the camera then?

(As the DEFENCE LAWYER scrambles for papers on his hands and knees BEA tries to help. She looks at one of the papers.)

BEA: Ooh! You're a legal man. Tell me, do you think the Wolves will go free, or are they heading for jail?

DEFENCE: Oh, they don't stand a chance. Those Wolves are going to jail for a long, long time... And I should know... because I'm their lawyer. Oh dear. I shouldn't have said that.

(The DEFENCE LAWYER goes to his desk in the courtroom. DEXTER has the camera ready. He gives BEA the thumbs up. BEA begins her report.)

BEA: Bea Bear here, with the big news story of the day. In a few short moments the –

(Enter TOMMY THIN, running. He looks alarmed. He points offstage.)

BEA: CUT! Excuse me, but you just ruined my report.

TOMMY: Wolves! Wolves! WO-O-O-OLVES!!

BEA: What? Where?

(There is a brief flap. DEXTER, BEA and the DEFENCE LAWYER run around in panic, bumping into each other. Then they realise that TOMMY is laughing his head off.)

TOMMY: Fooled you!

(He runs off.)

BEA: Kids! I can't stand kids! Right, Dexter…

(DEXTER starts filming again.)

BEA: … In a few short moments the notorious Wolf gang will finally go on trial.

(Enter a CLEANER, a POLICEMAN, a CLERK, a few MEMBERS OF THE PUBLIC GALLERY, including POLLY FLINDERS and JOHN MUDDLECOMBE, who quietly take up their places in the courtroom. The CLEANER sweeps up right between BEA and the camera. She is cross but decides to roll with it.)

(Music for A GOOD CLEAN TRIAL starts in the background.)

BEA: You, sir?

(BEA thrusts the microphone at the CLEANER.

CLEANER: Me?

BEA: Yes, you. What's your opinion on this case?

CLEANER: Haven't got one. You see:

(The CLEANER sings.)

SONG - A GOOD CLEAN TRIAL

I'm cleanin'. Just cleanin'. Just cleanin'... That's all!
This place will be gleamin' in no time at all.

(The CLERK bustles upstage from one side, the POLICEMAN from the other. BEA collars the CLERK.)

BEA: Ah, you then. Maybe you can give us a statement.

CLERK: No time. No time.

(POLICEMAN sings.)
I can't believe my eyes!
Have you seen the crowd outside?

(CLERK sings.)
More like a football ground than a court of law.

(POLICEMAN sings.)
Everybody pushing, barging,
And the crowd just keeps enlarging,

(CLERK sings.)
Better let them in or they'll break down the door!

(POLICEMAN goes off to 'open the door'.)

BEA: I need someone I can get a comment from!

DEXTER: *(looking offstage)* How many do you want?

(As he says this, the POLICEMAN reverses in, pushed on, and totally outnumbered by the rest of the MEMBERS OF THE PUBLIC GALLERY, who sing as they come.)

(MEMBERS OF THE PUBLIC sing.)
Open up, let us through, let us in,
'Cos we wouldn't want to miss a single thing,
The excitement's mounting,
We're all counting out the minutes till the fun begins.
Budge along, make a space now would you?
'Cos we all want a very, very good view
When they finally put those Wolves away and make 'em pay for all their sins.

(EVERYONE *sings.*)
> We'll have a good clean fight
> Of wrong v. right,
> As fair as fair can be –
> And then we have no doubt,
> The judge will shout
> "We're going to lock-em-up, and throw away the key!"

BEA: Here comes the jury, Dexter. Get some shots!

(*From the other side the MEMBERS OF THE JURY enter in a stately procession. They sing.*)
> We are the Jury, we must decide,
> Who goes to jail and who goes free.
> We will be fair, we won't take a side,
> Just is a must for us to be...

(*Finally they all – PUBLIC, JURY, CLERK and CLEANER sing their verses together followed by the chorus.*)

(EVERYONE *sings.*)
> We'll have a good clean trial,
> And in a while
> Those wolves – will see
> That they are good and hooked!
> Their goose is cooked!
> And we all know just what the end will be-e-e!
> We're going to lock-em-up
> And throw away the ke-e-ey!

(*During the final chorus, DEXTER and BEA join the PUBLIC. BEA sits between POLLY FLINDERS and JOHN MUDDLECOMBE*)

CLERK: Court will rise! Is the Prosecutor here?

PROS: (*self-importantly*) Present, Your Honour!

CLERK: Is the Defence here?

CLERK: That's you.

DEFENCE: (*flustered*) Really? Oh... What was the question again?

CLERK: Are you here?!

DEFENCE: Oh, I see. Well then, I suppose... Yes. Yes, I think I am!

CLERK: I'm not so sure myself! *(to POLICEMAN)* Bring in the prisoners.

The POLICEMAN nips off. He comes back with the three wolves – BIG BAD, LITTLE BAD and KNUCKLES. A chorus of boos from the PUBLIC. DEXTER and BEA run across to the accused.

BEA: Wolves. Anything to say?

BIG BAD: We are the innocent victims of a terrible injustice, and we will prove it!

LITTLE: *(over-dramatic)* We have been stitched up like kippers, and we will fight this every inch of the way!

KNUCK: *(leaning right into the microphone)* Can I just say hello to my mum and anybody that knows me?

CLERK: Order in court. Order in court! Now... who's missing...?

(The CLERK looks around. The POLICEMAN whispers in his ear.)

CLERK: Ladies and gentlemen of the court, it's the moment you've all been waiting for. Yes, here he is, the one, the only, please give it up for... his Honour... the Judge!

SONG - COURT WILL RISE

(JURY sings.)

When a crime's been committed and it's caused a shock,
And a person's been arrested and they're sitting in the dock,
When you need someone as steady as a lighthouse rock,
All rise for the wise old Judge.

He's as brave and impressive as a Superman,
All the crooks need do is look at him and they know they stand
Just the same chance as a snowball in a frying pan!
So I bid you rise,
As the case he tries,
He's the wise... old... Judge!

(The JUDGE enters. He is swaggering like a pop star as he receives the adulation of the crowd. He ignores his seat, and comes straight to the front of the stage.)

SONG - I AM THE JUDGE

(JUDGE sings, backed by CLERK, DEFENCE and PROSECUTION)
When I was bouncing on my mother's knee,
She looked at me and asked me straight –
"When you grow up what would you like to be?"
Well, I did not hesitate.
I said "I want to be a Judge, Ma,"
She said:

(MEMBERS of the JURY sing.)
"Why would that be, son?"

(JUDGE sings.)
I said, "I'd love to be a Judge, Ma –
Because a Judge's job looks SO MUCH FUN!"

'Cos everybody stands up when I walk in the room;
I get a cool red robe as well,
And if a witness don't appeal to me,
Well, I can send that sucker to the cells.
I get a hammer that's all my own,
And I can bang it on the table till the cows come home,
Oh Mama can't you see, that it's great to be a Judge.

I worked hard all night and every day -
And then I went to law-school too.
And in a little while, I'm glad to say
That my childhood dream came true.
And as a Judge I was appointed,
I got the wig and robe and all,
And I was not disappointed
Because from that day I've been HAVING A BALL!

'Cos everybody stands up when I walk in the room,
Oh it's a job that's heaven sent,
And if a lawyer won't appeal to me,
Well I can scowl and say "YOU'RE IN CONTEMPT!"
I really love the work I do –
Now people, ask yourselves honestly – wouldn't you?
It must be plain to see that it's great to be a Judge.
Whoa, whoa, whoa,
People, can't you see?

I've got the best little job in legal history,
I'm thankful every day that I get to play – the Judge.
I'm happy as a clam, because I am – the Judge!

My word is law – I have the power,
I get to send a guy to jail about once an hour!

It ought to be a crime,
That it's so-o-o fine – to be a Judge… to be a Judge… to be a Judge…
SILENCE IN COURT!

(JUDGE sits down in seat and carries on as if nothing has happened.)

JUDGE:	Okay. Let's get on with it.
CLERK:	*(to the WOLVES)* You are the Wolves?
WOLVES:	*(all together)* Yes.
CLERK:	You are charged with being criminals, a public menace, and a generally bad lot. How do you plead?
BIG BAD:	Eh?
CLERK:	How do you plead?
KNUCK:	I usually do this…

(KNUCKLES drops to his hands and knees, wails to heaven, wraps his arms around the CLERK's knees and pleads for all he's worth. The other WOLVES just shrug.

JUDGE:	He means, are you guilty or not guilty?
KNUCK:	You should know. You're the judge.
JUDGE:	Do you think you did it?
KNUCK:	Er…
BIG BAD and LITTLE:	NO!
JUDGE:	Thank you! They plead not guilty. Who's the first witness?

(Suddenly TOMMY THIN runs out from the public gallery in apparent terror.)

TOMMY:	WOOOO-LF!!!!

(TOMMY points to the door.)

TOMMY: WOOOO-LF!

(Everyone dives for cover, or cowers – except the WOLVES. They are looking to see if friends have arrived. There is a frozen moment. Then TOMMY drops his terrified act, and laughs like a drain.)

TOMMY: Fooled you!

(Embarrassed and annoyed, the MEMBERS OF THE PUBLIC settle down again. TOMMY is sent off by the POLICEMAN.)

JUDGE: Don't I know him?

CLERK: Tommy Thin, m'lord. You fined him once for trying to fill a well.

JUDGE: But... that's not illegal.

CLERK: That depends on what you're trying to fill it with, my lord. He was trying to fill it with cats.

JUDGE: I see. Now perhaps we could have a first witness?

PROS: You could have three, m'lord. I call the three little Pigs!

(Enter STY and MALION, skipping to the music of 'Who's Afraid of the Big Bad Wolf', IRON walking. But the JUDGE bangs his gavel and wags a finger at them.)

PROS: You are three little Pigs?

THREE PIGS: *(timidly)* Yes.

DEFENCE: Objection.

JUDGE: Eh? Objection? What for?

DEFENCE: They're not that little, your Honour.

PROS: Very well, your Honour. *(to PIGS)* You are three medium-sized Pigs?

THREE PIGS: Yes.

PROS: Until recently, you lived at 3, 4, and 5, Woodland Avenue?

PIGS: Yes.

(MALION snivels. IRON and STY comfort him. PUBLIC react with sympathy.)

PROS: And at this time you were neighbours of the Wolves here, isn't that correct?

PIGS: Y-yes...

PROS: And were the Wolves good neighbours?

THREE PIGS: Not by the hair on our chinny chin chin!

(There is a pause. Everyone looks around, baffled.)

JUDGE: Could someone translate?

PROS: I believe they mean "No", your Honour. *(turns to the PIGS)*
                 Did these neighbours do anything in particular to upset you?

MALION: They... they... they blew our houses down!

IRON: One after the other... It was horrible... Horrible!

(Big reaction from MEMBERS OF THE PUBLIC.)

(DEFENCE Lawyer looks to the WOLVES. He shrugs helplessly.)

BIG BAD: We didn't touch their stupid houses.

DEFENCE: They didn't touch their stupid houses... er, I mean...
                 their houses.

LITTLE: Only the one.

DEFENCE: Only the one.

PROS: Aha! So you admit you wilfully destroyed one house!

BIG BAD: It was an accident!

LITTLE: We wanted to borrow some sugar.

KNUCK: We wanted to make some apple sauce. Apple sauce goes
                 lovely with...

(PIGS are horrified. IRON covers MALION'S ears.)

KNUCK: *(realising his blunder)* Er... some things!

LITTLE: All Knuckles did was knock on the door.

PROS: *(sneering)* Are you seriously asking this jury to believe that
                 he... *(points to KNUCKLES)* destroyed a house simply by
                 knocking at the door? Preposterous!

BIG BAD: Ask 'em what the house was made of, your Judgeship.

PROS:	Objection! Objection!
JUDGE:	What was it made of?
MALION:	*(mumbles)*
JUDGE:	Sorry. Could you speak up?
MALION:	Straw.
JUDGE:	Straw?
DEFENCE:	Straw?
JUDGE:	You built your house of straw?
BIG BAD:	So when Knuckles knocked... Pffft!
PROS:	Your Honour, all this does not explain how the other house was destroyed.
JUDGE:	*(to WOLVES)* Any explanation for that?

(The WOLVES shrug and look at the DEFENCE Lawyer who shrugs and looks at JUDGE.)

THREE PIGS:	THEY did it!
PROS:	I have no more questions, your Honour.
JUDGE:	*(to DEFENCE Lawyer)* And you?
DEFENCE:	Er... Do I?...Er... No. No, I don't think so... thank you.
BIG BAD:	But... but...
JUDGE:	Next witness!
PROS:	I call... Bo Peep!

(The call goes out. Enter BO PEEP with a small flock of SHEEP, who mill about and then settle down to one side.)

PROS:	You are Little Bo Peep?
DEFENCE:	OB-jection! She's not little. She's average-sized. He's only calling her 'little' to get the jury's sympathy. He wouldn't like it if I called them the three little Wolves!
PROS:	Well then. Perhaps if I call her... 'Average-sized' Bo Peep?

(The DEFENCE Lawyer shrugs and sits. The PROSECUTION Lawyer continues.)

PROS: You are... *(sighs)* Average-sized Bo Peep?

BO: Er... I am Bo Peep, yes.

PROS: And your job, Miss Peep?

BO: I am a shepherdess.

PROS: That's charming!

BO: Ooh! Where, where? I've always wanted to meet him...

PROS: No. Not 'Prince' Charming. I said, 'That's charming'... Your being a shepherdess, I mean.

BO: Oh. Sorry.

PROS: Could you tell us, Miss Peep, what happened to your flock on the afternoon of May 22nd this year?

BO: They were frightened half to death! That's what happened.

PROS: By whom were they frightened, Miss Peep?

BO: By *(pointing dramatically at the WOLVES)* these wolves!

(The PUBLIC react.)

WOLVES: *(variously)* Eh? Never! We never touched her sheep *(etc)*.

BO: Oh, it was horrible. One minute the flock was grazing in my meadow. Next minute, there were these wolves, drooling and howling and growling. My poor little lambs were petrified.

PROS: And was that all that happened that day, Miss Peep?

BO: No.

PROS: Could you tell the court the other thing that happened?

BO: My Eunice... *(she starts to sob)* My Eunice disappeared.

PROS: Eunice is your prize ewe, I believe.

BO: She was gorgeous. She'd won prizes all over the land.

PROS: And what do you think became of lovely, prize-winning Eunice,

Miss Peep?

BO: Isn't it obvious? (*pointing at the WOLVES*) They ate her!

(*The WOLVES deny it. The CROWD boos. BO collapses, sobbing dramatically.*)

PROS: And is it true, Miss Peep, that you were so distressed by your awful experience that you have sold the meadow in question?

(*The MEMBERS OF THE PUBLIC make sympathetic noises.*)

BO: (*tearfully*) I couldn't go back. There are just too many bad memories. I'd turned down an offer before, from Miss Terry, but... after that terrible day.... (*she cries.*)

LITTLE: It's not looking good, Big Bad.

BIG BAD: No. Looks like the whole court's united against us.

LITTLE: And so far it's United one, Wolves nil!

(*The DEFENCE Lawyer gets to his feet.*)

BIG BAD: Here, hold on, maybe Legal Eagle's got a plan...

DEFENCE: Miss Peep. This isn't the first time you have er... mislaid your flock... is it?

BO: I don't know what you mean!

DEFENCE: Really? I have here a copy of the *Once-Upon-a-Times* – the lost-and-found notices. (*reads*) Ahem – 'Little...(*significant look*) Bo Peep has lost her sheep, and doesn't know where to find them... reward offered.'

PROS: Objection! It doesn't matter how many sheep she lost in the past. It's all irrelevant.

KNUCK: What's her elephant got to do with this?

DEFENCE: Perhaps she simply lost her sheep – again – and decided to invent this wolf story to shift the blame?

PROS: (*sarcastic*) Honestly! Perhaps you'd like to ask the sheep!

DEFENCE: Thanks, I will. Call the sheep!

(*The SHEEP are called. They leave their places and mill about uselessly. Eventually they are herded into a group.*)

DEFENCE: You are Bo Peep's sheep?

(At first the SHEEP look to their leader, RAGLAN. As soon as he answers, they answer too.)

RAGLAN: Y-e-e-es!

ALL SHEEP: *(joining in)* Ye-e-es!

DEFENCE: And you say you were attacked by three wolves?

RAGLAN: Ye-e-e-s!

SHEEP 2:   Actually, four.

SHEEP 3:   Four?

SHEEP 4:   He's right. It was four.

SHEEP 3:   Oh, yes. Yes, it was four.

(The CROWD mutters. The PROSECUTION Lawyer jumps to his feet.)

PROS: They were all very frightened, your Honour... Probably they imagined there were four.

ALL SHEEP: *(variously)* Yeah. You're probably right. Our mistake.

PROS: So there were only three wolves?

SHEEP: Ye-e-es!

PROS: These three!

SHEEP: Y-e-e-e-s!

WOLVES: *(variously)* Hold on! That's not fair!

DEFENCE: It's not even your go!

PROS: Members of the jury, clearly we have here a vicious gang of wolves, who will stop at nothing, who are known to eat small, defenceless, furry creatures. *(RABBITS in the jury react.)* They have destroyed property, they have carried out unprovoked attacks on innocent pigs – they have even consumed a much-loved prize sheep...

(BO wails.)

PROS: It must be beyond all doubt by now that they are... GUILTY!

(The PROSECUTION Lawyer thumps the table. The DEFENCE Lawyer jumps, sending papers and stuff flying. He starts to scrabble around.)

DEFENCE: I wish you wouldn't do that!

JUDGE: *(to DEFENCE)* Is there anything you want to say?

(The DEFENCE Lawyer is now tangled up in his gown.)

DEFENCE: Sorry? Er.... What was that?

JUDGE: You have nothing more to say at all?

DEFENCE: Er... No thanks.

JUDGE: Are you sure?

DEFENCE: Quite sure, thank you...

(JUDGE turns to WOLVES, who are in shock. JUDGE shrugs helplessly.)

BIG BAD: Where did you find that lawyer, Knuckles? He's useless.

KNUCK: I don't understand. I went to the law school like you said.

BIG BAD: And you found the hardest-working person there?

KNUCK: Yeah. Most of 'em were just sitting around reading books, but he was out there, sleeves rolled up, and I've never seen cleaner windows.

(BIG BAD and LITTLE BAD groan.)

BIG BAD: Well, boys. We're in trouble now. The public hates us, the jury hates us, and our lawyer's a window cleaner. There's only one thing we can do now.

KNUCK: Eat the jury?

BIG BAD: No, Knuckles! We have to get everyone in this courtroom on our side.

KNUCK: There isn't much room here. Can't we go on their side?

LITTLE: He means – we have to get them to like us.

KNUCK: Oh, I see. *(pauses to scratch his head)* How are we going to do that, then?

BIG BAD: Leave everything to me. Er... Your Judgeship?

JUDGE: What do you want?

BIG BAD: With your permission, we'd like to say something.

JUDGE: Oh... very well!

(The WOLVES step into the centre. Everybody shrinks back a bit.)

BIG BAD: There's been a lot of talk about how we wolves like to eat little animals. Well that may be so, but it isn't the whole story! Allow us to explain...

SONG - WOLF SONG

(BIG BAD sings)
    Your Honour – Members of the Jury,
    When I see something small and furry,
    I get this rumbly feeling deep inside,
    And I get a sort of hunch I'm about to meet my lunch.
    It isn't pleasant, but it isn't Homicide!

    Because – I'm a wolf,
    It don't make me a sinner,
    Though it's true I'm partial to a bunny for dinner..
    But then I'm afraid, folks,
    It's the way I was made, folks.
    I'm not a cow, I couldn't chow on grass and, Hey!
    Maybe that's why I'm in the dock today!

(LITTLE BAD sings)
    A single kindly word my soul I'd gladly sell for,
    But every time I walk onto their land –

(KNUCKLES sings)
    The farmers all rush out to greet us with the twelve-bore,

(LITTLE BAD sings)
    They never even try to understand,

(BIG BAD sings)
    I wish I was cute,

(KNUCKLES sings)
    Like a cutey koala,

(LITTLE BAD sings)
    A koala they'd invite right into the parlour,

(*BIG BAD sings*)
>But no one equipped us, to digest eucalypytus,
>So I'm a carnivore just like my mum and dad.
>That is why everybody says I'm bad.

>Now let's be clear, I don't appear wearing sheep's clothing,
>I'm not ashamed of who or what I am.
>But everywhere I go, I just see hate and loathing,
>And all because I like a leg o' lamb!

(*SHEEP panic.*)

BIG BAD: (*aside*) Sorry…

(*BIG BAD sings*)
>But then I'm a wolf – I'm a stranger to love,
>But that doesn't mean I've done the things they're accusing me of.

(*All three WOLVES sing*)
>So please hear our cries, folks
>We're three innocent guys, folks!

(*KNUCKLES sings*)
>Oh, we may be pretty scary,

(*LITTLE BAD sings*)
>An' we're far from vegetarian,

(*All thee WOLVES sing*)
>But underneath, we're decent through and through.
>If you knew us, you would know that's true!

PROS: I'm sure we're all very touched. But it doesn't change the fact that you are GUILTY!

(*On the word 'GUILTY' the PROSECUTION lawyer bangs the table again. The DEFENCE lawyer jumps a mile.*)

JUDGE: Well, members of the jury. You've heard all the evidence. Now you must go away and decide on your verdict.

CLERK: Court will rise.

JUDGE: Take the prisoners down.

POLICE: Come on, you furry felons. Back to the cell.

(*BEA rushes forward to the WOLVES, DEXTER follows reluctantly.*)

BEA: Well, this is it, Wolves. What do you think your chances are?

(The WOLVES begin to weep, blowing their noses on enormous handkerchiefs.)

BEA: Hmmm. Look, I know you could do with a little bit of luck... So I want you to have this.

(BEA holds up her lucky paperclip.)

LITTLE: What's that?

BEA: It's my lucky paperclip.

BIG BAD: *(suspiciously)* Lucky paperclip?

BEA: Yeah. Look, I'm not saying I think you're innocent – but I'm not sure you're guilty either.

LITTLE: Everyone else thinks we are.

BEA: I know. That's why I thought you might find my lucky paperclip useful.

BIG BAD: Useful?

BEA: Yes. Like I said. It's lucky.

LITTLE: Oh, right. She means... Useful!

(LITTLE BAD nudges the other WOLVES.)

BIG BAD: Oh... RIGHT!

KNUCK: Oh... No, sorry. I still don't get it.

(BIG BAD puts the paperclip carefully in his pocket.)

BIG BAD: Never mind. We'll explain later. For now...Shhhhhhhh!

(The POLICEMAN has come nearer, slightly suspicious. The WOLVES give him big innocent smiles, then allow themselves to be led away.)

WOLVES: Thanks. See you soon. Really soon. *(they exit)*

(BEA goes to the DEFENCE Lawyer.)

BEA: So! How do you think it looks for your clients?

DEFENCE: I... that is... Oh, dear... Oh, deary deary me...

(He scoops up his papers and starts to scuttle off.)

BEA: As good as that, eh?

(Just before he leaves, the DEFENCE Lawyer turns.)

DEFENCE: The windows here are in a terrible state. I wonder if they need
                someone to clean them?

(DEFENCE Lawyer exits. Bea turns to the PROSECUTION Lawyer)

BEA: And you, sir. How did it go from your point of view?

PROS: Well, as a lawyer of many years standing, and taking into
                account all the legal technicalities, I think I would have to
                say... I won! I won! Nah nah ne nah nah! *(blows enormous
                raspberry)* Those wolves are TOAST!

BEA: Hmmm. Pretty confident then. Roll camera, Dexter.

*(There is a commotion on the other side of the stage. The POLICEMAN shoots out
of the wings and grabs the JUDGE. He whispers urgently in the JUDGE'S ear.)*

JUDGE: What? No!

(DEXTER swings the camera up, BEA lifts the microphone.)

BEA: This is Bea Bear at the Wolf trial, where there seems to be some
                new development. Your Honour, what seems to be the trouble?

JUDGE: I'd rather not say. We don't want a panic.

BEA: Why should there be a panic?

POLICE: Because the Wolves have escaped.

JUDGE: *(sarcastically)* Oh, well done!

(There is pandemonium. The PUBLIC scatter and leave.)

POLICE: We'd better tell the jury.

*(The JURY suddenly come straight through screaming and send the JUDGE and
the POLICEMAN spinning as they pass.)*

JUDGE: Don't bother. They know.

(The JUDGE stomps off, shaking his head. Suddenly, TOMMY THIN runs on.)

TOM: Wolf! Wolf! WOLFFFF!!!!!

BEA and DEX: Where?

(TOM points offstage.)

TOM: Wolf! There!

(BEA, the POLICEMAN and DEXTER look in the direction he's pointing.)

TOM: Ha ha! Fooled you!!

(TOM runs off. BEA and DEXTER and POLICEMAN are left alone.)

BEA: Right. *(to camera)* Exclusive. Dramatic news from the court where it's just been announced that the Wolves have escaped. *(She grabs the POLICEMAN.)* Exactly what happened?

POLICEMAN: Are we on television?

BEA: Yes.

POLICE: Gosh... Well... Bea.... Ahem... Hit would seem that the Wolves picked the lock hof their cell.

BEA: And how did they do that?

POLICE: We believe they had hinside help. I mean hinside the Court, obviously, not hinside the lock!

BEA: You mean –

POLICE: Yes, Bea. We are pretty sure that someone in the courtroom smuggled them the tool they used to hescape.

BEA: *(turning to camera)* Exclusive news, viewers. Not only have the Wolves escaped, but it seems they had assistance from someone in this very courtroom. Of course the question is, who could that person be? Which seemingly innocent bystander would smuggle these prisoners a... a... *(looks to POLICEMAN for help)*

POLICE: *(holding up a paperclip)* A paperclip.

BEA: Yes. What sort of cold-blooded sneak would have the nerve to slip these Wolves a... did you say paperclip?

DEXTER: *(lowering the camera)* Oops.

POLICEMAN: This very one!

BEA: Oh dear. Come on, Dexter. Let's get out of here!

POLICEMAN: Is that the end of the interview?

BEA: Er... yes.

DEXTER: What are you going to do now?

BEA: This. *(into news reporter mode)* This is Bea Bear, at the Woodland Courtroom, signing off... *(to DEXTER)* And now, we are going to find those Wolves if it's the last thing we do...

(BEA exits.)

DEXTER: Find the Wolves?

(DEXTER laughs at the ridiculousness of it, then suddenly stops.)

DEXTER: *We?*

END OF PART ONE

Part Two

A country scene suggested by a couple of framing tree trunks and a green 'tuffet'. BEA and DEXTER appear from different sides of the stage – perhaps BEA can come through the auditorium. They ask if people have seen the Wolves. They call. They look round corners. They end up on the stage.

BEA: Oh, Dexter! What am I going to do? I've helped the Wolves escape.

DEXTER: You didn't do it on purpose! Anyway, I thought you said they were innocent.

BEA: I said, I wasn't sure they were guilty.

(POLLY FLINDERS and JOHN MUDDLECOMBE appear to music of 'Little Polly Flinders'. MUDDLECOMBE is taking notes in a little notebook.)

POLLY: I'm glad you said that.

DEXTER
and BEA: Aaargh! Who are you?

POLLY: *(holding out a card)* Flinders is the name. Polly Flinders. This is John Muddlecombe.

DEXTER: *(reading a card)* ...Private Investigators.

POLLY: We heard what you said just now.

BEA: When I said 'helped', I didn't really mean 'helped'.

POLLY: About the Wolves being possibly innocent.

BEA: *(very relieved)* Oh, that!

POLLY: You see, we think so too. You couldn't call that a fair trial. Those sheep were quite sure at first that they saw four wolves, not three. The Wolves' lawyer should have picked up on that. But then, he was a complete...

MUDD: Window-cleaner?

BEA: Window-cleaner. How did you know that?

POLLY: We're private investigators.

MUDD: We notice things.

POLLY: Exactly, John. So anyway, we've decided to do a bit of digging.

MUDD: And we thought you could help us!

BEA: We don't want to get involved in this. It's not our problem.

POLLY: Fair enough.

BEA: Come on, Dex.

(As they are leaving, Polly calls out.)

POLLY: By the way – lost any nice paperclips lately?

(BEA and DEXTER scuttle back.)

BEA: How did you know about that?

POLLY: We're private investigators.

MUDD: We notice things.

BEA: I wasn't trying to help them escape.

POLLY: But it may be a good thing that they have. It gives us a chance to prove them innocent. If we can, the whole paperclip thing will be yesterday's news. No one will even remember it.

DEXTER: She's right, Bea.

BEA: Where do we start?

POLLY: Excellent. John has an idea.

MUDD: I think we should talk to Bo Peep again.

BEA: Well? What are we waiting for?

(They all march off. Immediately, the sound of massed baa-ing is heard. BO PEEP enters, looking sad. She sits on the tuffet and all the sheep sit around her.)

BO: Okay, settle down now. It's time to take the register. Angora? Arran? Baabera? Fleecity?

POLLY
and MUDD: *(offstage)* Miss Peep? Miss Peep?

(POLLY, MUDDLECOMBE, BEA and DEXTER arrive to the music of 'Old John Muddlecombe Lost his Cap'. They pick their way through the seated sheep, and finally get to BO.)

BO: Can I help you?

POLLY: We're Muddlecombe and Flinders, private investigators.

BO: I saw you in the courtroom. Tell me, have they caught those terrible Wolves yet?

BEA: Er... no.

DEXTER: Nice meadow.

BO: I know. I'll be sorry to leave it.

MUDD: Yes, you sold it to... Miss Terry. Is that right? Can you tell us anything about her?

BO: I told all I know in court.

POLLY: I know, but if you could go over it once more. For us. It's really very important.

BO: Oh... very well... That day was a day like any other...

SONG - THE ONLY EWE THAT I ADORE

(BO PEEP sings)
>I led my flock *(SHEEP sing, That's us)* to play out in the meadow,
>A thing I've done a hundred times before.
>But little did I know that day out in the meadow
>I'd lose the only ewe that I adore.

(SHEEP sing.)
>She told her team to let off steam down in the meadow,

(BO sings.)
>I closed my eyes,
>Five minutes – nothing more,
>I woke from sleep to find no sheep down in the meadow,
>I'd lost the only ewe that I adore.

>Oh I hollered and I whistled, I even sang their favourite song,
>I thought the only crook in town was in my hand – but I was wrong.

>I put a sign on every tree out in the meadow,
>I asked around –
>I went from door to door,
>But not one peep about my sheep was ever said – Oh!
>I'd lost the only ewe that I adore:

>Oh I hollered and I whistled, and I searched both near and far –
>And it was as the moon was rising that I heard a plaintive:

(SHEEP sing.)
>Baaa-aa-aa!

(BO PEEP sings.)
>And pale and thin my sheep crept in to the meadow,
>So scared, their wool was even whiter than before,
>But now I cry most every day…
>'Cos there's one still M.I.A…
>I've lost the only ewe that I… a… dore…

(SHEEP sing.)
>Baaaaaa–aaaaaaaaaaah!

POLLY: Thank you, Miss Peep. And this sheep that disappeared?

BO: Eunice. My bestest, number one, most adorable sheep in the
              whole wide world...

(BO wails. MUDDLECOMBE takes hanky out of his cap and offers it.)

MUDD: Correct me if I'm wrong here, Miss Peep – but you didn't actually see the Wolves at all. Is that right?

BO: Er... not exactly with-my-own-eyes see them, no. But *they* did! Ask them.

(BO indicates the SHEEP.)

MUDD: *(to the SHEEP)* Right. Who's the leader around here?

(RAGLAN puts his hand up. The others all look at him, then put their hands up too. MUDDLECOMBE shakes his head. RAGLAN speaks.)

RAGLAN: *(to SHEEP)* Stop copying, you lot! *(to POLLY and MUDDLECOMBE)* I'm Raglan. They all follow me.

MUDD: Okay, Raglan. On the day that Eunice... disappeared...

(BO wails. BEA and POLLY comfort her.)

MUDD: You told Miss Peep that you were attacked by wolves. Is that true?

RAGLAN: Yes.

SHEEP: Yes.

MUDD: How many wolves were there?

RAGLAN: Four.

SHEEP: That's right. Four.

(One LAMB at the back isn't so sure.)

LAMB: Three, Rag. That nice man in court said there were only three. Remember?

SHEEP: *(nodding)* That's right. Only three.

DEXTER: Oh, brother. This isn't getting us anywhere.

MUDD: Never mind what the man in court said. Think. This is very important. How many were there... exactly?

(All the SHEEP look at each other and finally nod.)

SHEEP:	Four.
MUDD:	Very interesting. *(he writes in his notebook)* And what did these four wolves look like?
RAGLAN:	Hairy.
SHEEP:	Hairy.
LAMB:	Scary.
SHEEP:	Scary.
RAGLAN:	And round.
MUDD:	Round?
SHEEP:	Round?
RAGLAN:	Yeah, round. Small and round.
MUDD:	Hmmmmm. *(makes a note)*
DEXTER:	Not bad. Considering they've only got one RAM of memory between them.
BEA:	Be quiet, Dex.
MUDD:	*(to RAGLAN)* Anything else?

(There is a silence. A bit of shuffling.)

MUDD:	Raglan?
LAMB:	Tell him, Rag.
MUDD:	Tell me what?
LAMB:	Raglan got a tail.
BEA:	What?
RAGLAN:	It was a souvenir. That's all.
BO:	Raglan! I never knew!
SHEEP:	He hid it behind his ba-a-ack!
MUDD:	*(taking notes)* She left them alone... and he came home... dragging a tail behind him!

RAGLAN: Look, it's so bo-ooo-ring, being a sheep. A wolf attack is pretty big news. So when I saw this tail lying about afterwards, I thought, "I'll keep that, to help me remember this day!"

BO: That's the last time you watch Mr Benn!

POLLY: Could we see this tail, Raglan?

BO: Stop acting sheepish, Raglan. Show them.

(RAGLAN reluctantly brings out a wolf tail. POLLY and MUDDLECOMBE take it to one side.)

MUDD: Take a look.

DEXTER: Hey. This isn't real!

RAGLAN: It is!

POLLY   It's not. Look.

RAGLAN: Blow me! I've been fleeced!

(BEA takes the tail, turns it about and examines it minutely.)

BEA: Look. Here's a label. I can't quite...

(MUDDLECOMBE looks through his glasses.)

MUDD: *(reads)* Mother Hubbard's Cupboard. Fancy Dress for All Occasions.

BEA: Right. Let's go and talk to her.

POLLY: You go. I want to check out the Wolves' other neighbours. See what they say about this whole business.

BEA: Okay.

BO: Will you be wanting anything else?

POLLY: No thank you, Miss Peep. You and your sheep have been a great help.

BO: You're very welcome. Come on, flock. This way...

(The SHEEP start to file offstage.)

RAGLAN: Bo? Can me and a few of the boys go for a gambol in the top field?

BO: Certainly not, Raglan. You know I don't approve of gambolling!

(Exit BO and all the SHEEP)

POLLY: Right. You two go and see what you can find at Mother Hubbard's, and we'll meet up later. Come on, John.

MUDD: Wait... I need my cap. Where's my cap?

POLLY, BEA
and DEXTER: You've got it on your head!

MUDD: What, again? Sorry.

(BEA and DEXTER split up from POLLY and MUDDLECOMBE and leave the stage. From behind a tree, PIG MALION appears, swathed in a coat, collar turned up. He tiptoes down, checking the others have gone. He is unsure of which group to follow but finally plumps for MUDDLECOMBE and FLINDERS. Follows them off and exits stage left.)

Enter MR MARY stage right, carrying a SOLD sign, to the music of 'Mary, Mary Quite Contrary'. MRS MARY follows with a suitcase.

MRS MARY: Well, I must say I'll miss the old place.

MR MARY: I know, dear.

MRS MARY: Especially Mary's garden.

MR MARY: All those silver bells...

MRS MARY: And cockle shells...

MR MARY: And...

MRS MARY: *(warning)* Brian!

MR MARY: Hurry up Mary! The van's waiting.

(Enter MUDDLECOMBE and FLINDERS, out of puff.)

POLLY: Mr and Mrs Mary?

MRS MARY: Yes? Hello. Are you the new owners? I hope you'll be as happy here as we've been...

POLLY: New owners? Have you sold this place?

MUDD: Is that because of trouble with the Wolves?

MRS MARY:	Dear me, no. Lovely boys, the Wolves.
MR MARY:	Noisy eaters.
MRS MARY:	Very noisy eaters. But lovely boys. No. We're selling because we had a marvellous offer. You're not the new owners, then? Only we've never met them.
MR MARY:	It was all done by letter, you see.
POLLY:	I see. Well we're not them, I'm afraid. We're private investigators. *(hands them a card)* We wanted to ask you about the three Pigs. You know – the house flattening business?
MR MARY:	Terrible business. Terrible.
MUDD:	Did you see what happened?
MR MARY:	Oh yes.
MRS MARY:	Not that we're nosy.
MR MARY:	No, no no no. Not nosy at all. No.
MRS MARY:	But we saw EVERYTHING!
MR MARY:	Course it should never have been there in the first place. I said to my wife, didn't I dear? I said they've no business allowing a straw house there. I mean, it's a fire risk. There are rules…
MUDD:	Yes quite… So you saw the wolf… er… *(looks at notes)* Knuckles – do what exactly?
MR MARY:	He knocked on the door. That's all. And the whole lot came down.
POLLY:	And what about the other house. The… stick house?
MR MARY:	Oh yes. That one went too.
MRS MARY:	Terrible. I'm glad I wasn't there to see it.
MR MARY:	I said to my wife… didn't I dear?…. I said… There goes the neighbourhood. The council will never clear that lot up, I said…
POLLY:	You mean… you didn't see the Wolves do it?
MRS MARY:	Wolves? Oh no. But we know they did it.

MUDD: How do you know?

MR MARY: Er... I think the Pigs told us.

MRS MARY: Yes, they did.

(MUDDLECOMBE makes a note.)

POLLY: That's very interesting.

(MARY MARY enters to the music of 'Mary had a little lamb'. Following her is a sheep, EUNICE. EUNICE takes one look at POLLY and MUDDLECOMBE, and panics. Bleating in alarm, she runs to the back of the stage)

MRS MARY: Now do get that sheep organised, Mary.

MARY: *(calling)* Come on Eunice. Nobody's going to hurt you, you silly... ewe!

MUDD and
POLLY: *(looking at each other)* Eunice?

POLLY: Are you Mary? Mary Mary?

MARY: No!

MUDD: But your mother called you Mary?

MARY: She didn't!

POLLY: She did!

MRS MARY: Sorry. She's a bit contrary.

MR MARY: Very contrary, as it happens.

MUDD: *(writing it down)* Mary Mary... quite... con...trary...

POLLY: Mary, how long have you had this sheep?

(MARY folds her arms and clams up. EUNICE imitates her.)

MR MARY: Not long. She found it. Didn't you dear?

MRS MARY: It was a stray.

MUDD: A stray sheep?

EUNICE: I'm not going back, you know!

MUDD: Going back where?

EUNICE: To her. To Bo Peep.

POLLY: So you are the missing sheep.

MUDD: You mean you weren't eaten by wolves!

EUNICE: No. But in all that confusion, I saw my chance to escape.

POLLY: Escape from what?

EUNICE: The pressure. You don't know what it was like. Day after day, having to be the best. Sheepdip twice a week. Manicures. Hours in curlers. Entered for stupid competitions all the time. It was a nightmare. I've got a new life now, with Mary. She likes me for who I am. I'm even going to school.

MUDD: A lamb...?

POLLY: In school...?

MUDD: Isn't that against the rule?

MARY: She follows me. What can I do?

POLLY: Listen, Eunice. I really think you should let Bo know that you're safe. But we're not here to take you back.

EUNICE: You're not? Great!

POLLY: I just need to ask you. Do you remember anything about the wolves that attacked your flock that day?

EUNICE: Er... there were four of them... they were small and round-looking... and... oh, and one of them had a cap.

MUDD: A cap?

EUNICE: Yeah. A silly thing. With a tassle.

MUDD: (turning to Polly) A wolf? In a cap? Any of our wolves wear caps?

POLLY: Not that I've seen.

(MUDDLECOMBE makes a note. Sound of a car horn offstage.)

MR MARY: Now, into the van you two.

(Exit MARY, EUNICE and MR MARY.)

MRS MARY: *(to POLLY)* We really should go.

MUDD: Just one more thing, Mrs Mary. Who did you sell the house to?

MRS MARY: Oh, now let me think. It was a Mr... Mr... What was his name? Byars. Yes. that was it. Mr E. Byars.

(MUDDLECOMBE notes it down.)

POLLY: Well, thanks for your help. Bye.

MRS MARY: Bye... bye... *(car horn sounds again)* All right, I'm coming! *(exits)*

POLLY: Well, John. This case just gets more and more interesting. I wonder how Bea and Dexter are getting on...

(Exit POLLY and MUDDLECOMBE. PIG MALION comes out of hiding, looks anxiously after them, and then follows, trying to make contact on his radio.)

MALION: Middle Back to Bacon Leader. Come in Bacon Leader...

(PIG MALION also goes off. To the tune of 'Old Mother Hubbard' a shop counter appears stage left with a sign on the front that reads MOTHER HUBBARD'S CUPBOARD. BEA and DEXTER enter centre stage, and go over to counter. Sound effect of a shop bell tinkling.)

BEA: Hello?

DEXTER: Anybody in? Mrs Hubbard?

(MOTHER HUBBARD pops up from behind counter.)

MOTHER: Call me Mother. Hello dearies. If you were looking for costumes, I'm afraid the cupboard's bare. I've sold everything.

DEXTER: You mean you've got no costumes at all?

MOTHER: Sorry. If you'd come five minutes ago, I had a skeleton suit left. Ideal for Halloween. But even that's gone now. Nothing left, not even a bone.

(Sound of dog whimpering offstage)

MOTHER: Oh be quiet, Trixie!

BEA: Actually it wasn't a bone we were after. We wondered if you recognised this?

(BEA hands over the tail.)

MOTHER: Oh yes. That's from one of my wolf costumes. They've gone too, I'm afraid. Everything's gone. I'm selling up, you see.

BEA: Really?

MOTHER: I got a really good offer. From a Miss O'Nemus. Anne, I think her name was. Offered me much more than the old place is worth. I wanted to thank her in person, but the whole thing's been done through lawyers. I've never even met Miss O'Nemus.

DEXTER: Yeah. Very interesting... Now about these wolf costumes...

MOTHER: Oh, them. Well I had four made. Special order. Lovely outfits too. Just like the real thing. Only smaller, of course... and...

DEXTER: Round?

MOTHER: That's right, dearie.

BEA: Can you remember who you made them for?

MOTHER: Ooh, now you're asking.

(MOTHER HUBBARD opens a book and runs her finger down the page.)

MOTHER: Here we are... Krett. Arthur C. Krett. Funny looking chap he was. Little, with a big red beard... and a cap. Bought them, and a... a pig mask, I think it was....

DEXTER: A cap?

MOTHER: Yes. A funny little cap. With a tassle. I couldn't help noticing. Me being in the costume business and all.

BEA: Well, thank you, Miss... er... Mother. You've been very helpful.

MOTHER: That's all right, dearie.

(Sound of dog barking offstage.)

MOTHER: All right, Trixie, all right! Mummy's coming!

(MOTHER HUBBARD exits, taking the counter with her.)

BEA: I don't know what to make of all this.

DEXTER: Well, we're not detectives are we? Why not let Muddlecombe and Flinders sort it out?

BEA: Good idea. Let's go.

(BEA and DEXTER go offstage. The stage is empty for a moment. Maybe a musical interlude as the trees are brought back in. Then BEA, DEXTER, MUDDLECOMBE and FLINDERS all enter. MUDDLECOMBE has his notebook out.)

POLLY: Good work, everyone. I must say this case is getting very interesting. Wolf costumes for four!

BEA: Not three!

POLLY: I think we can safely say that our Wolves are innocent. Someone dressed up as them to attack Bo Peep's sheep, knowing that the Wolves would get the blame.

BEA: But why?

MUDD: There are a few more unanswered questions too. We have two reports of caps.

DEXTER: Both with tassles...

POLLY: And Bo Peep, the Marys, and Mother Hubbard... all of them selling up.

BEA: Yes, but that's just coincidence... Isn't it?

POLLY: Is it?

BEA: Surely. They've all sold to different people – Miss Terry, Miss O'Nemus, Mr Byars...

DEXTER: Hang on. Let me see that list! *(reads it over)* Miss Terry... Misterry.... Mystery!

POLLY: Miss Anne O'Nemus... Anne Onnemus...

BEA: Anonymous!

MUDD: Mr E. Byars...

ALL: Mystery Buyers!

BEA: Mystery, Anonymous, Mystery Buyers. They're all made-up names!

POLLY: Someone has been buying up property around here, using these names to keep the whole thing a secret.

DEXTER: That reminds me – the bloke that ordered the wolf suits from Mother Hubbard...

BEA: Arthur Krett.

DEXTER: Arthur C. Krett.

MUDD: A.C. Krett.

POLLY: A secret!

MUDD: So someone ordered wolf costumes...

DEXTER: Using a fake name...

POLLY: And then used those costumes to frighten Miss Peep's sheep, and make her sell her meadow.

MUDD: I'd say it's a fair bet that the person who ordered the wolf suits is the same person who's buying the land!

BEA: Hey! If they can dress as wolves to frighten Bo Peep... could they have done the same thing to frighten off the three Pigs? Maybe they flattened those houses?

MUDD: It's possible!

POLLY: Ah, but Knuckles admitted he knocked down the straw place.

DEXTER: Yeah. As an accident... But what if the real villains heard about that, and decided to wreck the other house the following night? The Wolves were bound to get the blame. The Pigs are frightened into selling up. The Wolves go to jail, and bingo – their land is available too. It's perfect! *(to audience)* I hope you're all following this!

POLLY: I say we pay the Pigs a visit and ask them some questions...

(ALL exit. Enter PIG MALION. Speaks urgently into his walkie-talkie.)

MALION: Middle Back to Bacon Leader. Middle Back to Bacon Leader. Come in Bacon Leader... *(Squawk from walkie talkie.)* Visitors heading your way. Repeat – visitors heading your way! *(exits)*

(Short musical interlude. A version of 'Teddybears' Picnic'...ending in the rat-tat-tat of a door-knocker. Voices are heard offstage.)

STY: Wh-wh-who is it?

BEA: It's Bea Bear, Mr Pig. From WXTV News. I wonder if I could ask you a few questions.

STY: I... I don't know...

BEA: Please, Mr Pig. It'll only take a few minutes.

STY: Well... All right.

(Sound effects of bolts being drawn, locks being unlocked, chains being run out. PIG IRON and PIG STY come in, followed by BEA, MUDDLECOMBE, POLLY and DEXTER.)

DEXTER: That's a lot of security.

IRON: *(timidly)* I'm sorry. My brothers and I are very nervous these days.

STY: *(fearful)* It's those Wolves. Those terrible, terrible Wolves. They've escaped you know...

BEA: Er... yes. We know.

STY: They did it. They did it all...

(STY starts to wipe his brow with his hankie. He is a bundle of nerves.)

DEXTER: Well actually... *(stops as BEA gags him with her hand)*

IRON: There now. *(To BEA and DEXTER)* He's still very upset.

POLLY: I just wanted to ask you and your brothers... Where's your other brother by the way?

STY and IRON: Out.

POLLY: I just wanted to ask, before the stick house was blown down, did anyone try to buy your land?

(STY looks at IRON. IRON shakes his head. STY joins in.)

STY: No.

POLLY: You're absolutely positive? No one asked you to sell, or tried to get you to move out?

IRON: No.

BEA: Are you sure?

STY: Of course we're sure. *(breaks down)* Why are you asking these questions, when the real criminals have escaped? My brothers and I are terrified to even go out!

DEXTER: I thought you said your other brother *was* out!?

STY: I... I... *(starting to rant)* Am I on trial here? Did I do anything? NO! Why are you even here? You should be out chasing those big, bad, brutally beastly Wolves! Not coming around bullying innocent Pigs! *(breaks down)*

IRON: I think you'd better go.

POLLY: Yes. Yes. Sorry. Come on, everyone.

(POLLY, MUDDLECOMBE, BEA and DEXTER exit, falling over themselves. PIG STY and PIG IRON are left alone.)

STY: How was I?

IRON: Very hammy!

STY: Why, thank you.

IRON: Now get those models. Mr Big-Pig will be here soon.

(PIG STY and PIG IRON exit. POLLY, MUDDLECOMBE, BEA and DEXTER reappear on the other side.)

BEA: Well, Polly? What do you say now?

POLLY: I don't know. I was so sure my theory was right. But if no one tried to buy their land... we're back to square... what on earth is that noise?

(There is a build-up of chanting and crowd noise. TOMMY THIN bursts in.)

TOM: Wolf! Wolf!

(TOMMY THIN runs off again. Moments later the PUBLIC from the trial appear. They are now a LYNCH MOB They have the THREE WOLVES tied up.)

MOB: They're big – they're hairy, They're sinister and scary, You'd best be very wary of a wolf!

DEXTER: What's going on?

LEADER: We caught them. We caught the Wolves!

BEA: And what are you planning to do with them?

MOB: *(chanting)* Chop them into little pieces, Tie them to a tree! Throw 'em down the nearest well..

LONE VOICE: Or eat them for our tea!

(MOB react with a mass 'Eugh!')

LEADER: No, no, no. We're taking them to court.

DEXTER: *(pointing back the way they've come)* But court's that way.

LEADER: So it is...

DEXTER: You weren't going to take them back at all, were you?

(MOB look sheepish.)

POLLY: What if I told you they were innocent?

MOB: Boo! Rubbish! Whose side are you on?

MUDD: She's right. We've been doing some investigating and...

LEADER: Well, if they're innocent... Who's guilty?

POLLY: We... we don't know...

MOB: Chop 'em into little pieces, tie 'em to a tree.

BEA: No wait! You see, someone's been secretly buying up the whole valley. If we can find out who that person is, we might know who's been trying to frame these Wolves!

BIG BAD: Hey! Didn't someone try to buy our house not so long ago Knuckles?

KNUCK: Oh, yeah. You're right. Nothing happened though. I lost the letter.

LEADER: A likely story. You're the Wolves! Everybody knows you're guilty. Everybody knows you're bad!

MOB: Chop 'em into little pieces...

POLLY:	STOP! I'm sure we can crack this case. We just need a bit more time.
LEADER:	How long?
POLLY:	Fifteen minutes?
DEXTER:	*(horrified)* Fifteen minutes!
LEADER:	Right. Fifteen minutes.

(The MOB march off with the WOLVES. POLLY, MUDDLECOMBE, BEA and DEXTER go into a huddle over MUDDLECOMBE'S notebook. PIG MALION appears from hiding and whispers into a walkie-talkie.)

DEXTER:	*(still horrified)* Fifteen minutes?
POLLY:	I was under pressure.
MALION:	Middle Back to Bacon Leader. Middle Back to Bacon Leader. Hello? Hello?

(PIG MALION returns to his hiding place. POLLY, MUDDLECOMBE, BEA and DEXTER come out of their huddle.)

POLLY:	There's something distinctly fishy going on here!
BEA:	I know exactly what you mean... *(pauses)* What *do* you mean, exactly?
POLLY:	Why hasn't this anonymous gang tried to buy the three Pigs' houses?
DEXTER:	Why should they?
MUDD:	Because they've bought everywhere else in this entire area. *(referring to notes)* The Marys' house...
BEA:	Sold.
MUDD:	Mother Hubbard's shop...
DEXTER:	Sold.
MUDD:	Bo Peep's meadow...
POLLY:	Sold.

BEA: And the Pigs' houses.

MUDD: And the Wolves say they had an offer...

POLLY: But the Pigs were quite definite that they haven't.

BEA: Let's face it...

DEX and POLLY: We're stumped.

SONG - WE HAVEN'T GOT A CLUE

(BEA sings)   We've been the most effective of detectives,
(POLLY sings)   I think we've made a really cracking team,
(MUDD sings)   We've done a lot of sleuthing and we're happy to proclaim
                 That we have solved the case...
(DEX sings)   Apart from knowing who's to blame!
(POLLY sings)   Yes, that's the piece that's missing from the puzzle
(BEA sings)   It's got us in a tizz...
(MUDD sings)   A flap...
(DEX sings)   A stew.
(POLLY sings)   Because although we've got a lot,
(DEX and
MUDD sing)   There's just one thing we haven't got,
(BEA sings)   A little thing that means a lot
(ALL sing)   WE HAVEN'T GOT A CLUE!

(MUDD sings)   We've talked to every witness we can think of,
(POLLY sings)   To find out who's been telling porky pies.
(BEA sings)   We've asked a lot of questions
(DEX sings)   And we're sure you will agree
(ALL sing)   That things round here are not the way
                 that they appear to be!
(BEA sings)   We've gathered lots of evidence and info;
(MUDD sings)   Collected all the facts and figures too!
(POLLY sings)   But though I know we're getting hot,
(POLLY and
MUDD sing)   There's just one thing we haven't got,
(BEA, POLLY
and
MUDD sing)   To fill that little empty spot –
(ALL sing)   WE HAVEN'T GOT A CLUE!

(BEA *sings*)   It's making us frustrated,

(DEX *sings*)   It's driving me insane,

(MUDD *and*
POLLY *sing*)   The facts are all collated,

(BEA *sings*)   The answer's in here somewhere,

(ALL *sing*)   So let's look at it again!

(*They all crowd round the notebook*)

(ALL *sing*)   We are the most effective of detectives,
The best investigators in the land.
We haven't left a stone unturned in searching for the truth,

(MUDD *sings*)   A flap...

(DEX *sings*)   The only thing that's missing is a single shred of proof!

(MUDD *sings*)   We've got it all in writing in my notebook.
Each piece of gen is in its proper place.

(ALL *sing*)   But though we know we have a lot,
We need one thing to crack the plot

(DEX *sings*)   The only thing that we haven't got

(DEX, MUDD
and POLLY
sing)   We haven't got a

(BEA *sings*)   Wait!

(DEX, MUDD
and POLLY
sing)   What?

(BEA *sings*)   It's just... I think...At last I see...
If she... and they... and them... and he...
That only leaves... it has to be...

(DEX, MUDD
and POLLY
sing)   What? What? What?

(BEA *sings*)   I think we've cracked the case!

(ALL *sing*)   Yes!

BEA: I see it all now. I know what's happened.

POLLY: Tell us!

BEA: No time to explain. Just follow me.

DEXTER: Follow you where?

BEA: (*leaving*) To the Pigs' house!!

(PIG MALION scuttles off, shaking his walkie-talkie. PIG STY and PIG IRON enter from the opposite side carrying a large model of an awesome-looking 'reactor' style complex.)

STY: I still think the warehouses should be here.

IRON: It can't be there, because that's where the main factory building is going.

STY: But you want to put the storage as near as you can to the new motorway! It's easier for all those big smelly lorries.

(Walkie-talkie crackles. PIG IRON picks it up.)

IRON: Bacon Leader here. Is that you, Middle Back? What? Stop squealing and speak up Middle Back – I can't understand a word you're saying... *(more crackle)* Mr Big, in trouble? No? Then who? Who's in trouble?

(POLLY, MUDDLECOMBE and BEA burst in.)

BEA: You! That's who!

STY: Oh! What are you doing here? It's the Wolves you should be after. Those hairy, scary, scheming...

POLLY: Save all that for the Judge! You Pigs made one big blunder. You told us that no one was after your land. Well, there was only one explanation for that. Mr A.C.Krett, Miss Terry, Anne O'Nemus, Mr E. Byars. They were all names made up by you, so that you could secretly buy the rest of the valley.

(DEXTER comes in, with PIG MALION in tow. PIG STY edges offstage.)

DEXTER: Look what I found skulking about outside!

MALION: Sorry, Bacon Leader. I tried to warn you!

BEA: But why. Why would three little... sorry, medium-sized Pigs want to buy this whole valley?

MUDD: *(indicating model)* This is why!

BEA: *(reading label)* 'Four Pigs Artificial Pork Pie and Fake Bacon Works.' Four pigs?

(They all turn to PIG IRON. PIG STY reappears with a large bin bag.)

DEXTER: And where do you think you're going?

STY: Oh, just putting the rubbish out.

DEXTER: Fair enough. Just checking.

BEA: Wait! Let me see that!

(BEA empties the bag. Wolf ears, snouts and tails fall out. So does the red beard. Also a list.)

DEXTER: Wolf suits… a red beard… And just look at this: Red Riding Hood… The three Billy Goats Gruff… Georgy Porgie… they'd done deals with everyone in the valley!

STY: *(panicking)* It wasn't our idea. He made us do it!

IRON: Be quiet, you fool.

POLLY: Who made you do it?

STY: Mr Big-pig! He's coming here now. He's the one you want!

DEXTER: He's right! There's someone coming!

PIGS: *(all)* Mr Big-pig!!

POLLY: Everybody hide!

(POLLY, MUDDLECOMBE, BEA and DEXTER hide. PIG MALION, PIG STY and PIG IRON stand petrified. Enter TOMMY THIN in pig mask – fatter-faced than the others – with a tasselled cap on top.)

TOMMY
(as BIG-PIG):   Hello. What's the matter with you?

BEA: Get him!

(There is a chase and a struggle. Finally they catch BIG-PIG (TOMMY. and pull off his mask. The PIGS are as surprised as the others.)

PIGS: *(all)* You're not a pig! You're… you're…

(DEXTER takes the tasselled cap from the mask, and puts it on top of TOMMY's head. Now they recognise him.)

MUDD: Tommy Thin!

DEXTER: The kitty-dunker! So it was you all along!

TOMMY: Who were you expecting? Scooby Doo?

POLLY: Well, well, well. Little Tommy Thin!

TOMMY: Don't call me Little! I hate that. You won't be calling me little when I've bulldozed this valley and built my factory. I'll be Big Tommy Thin then! And you'll all be sorry!

POLLY: There isn't going to be any factory, Tommy Boy. And you're the one who's going to be sorry, when the Judge has finished with you! The funny thing is, you'd probably have got away with the whole scheme if there had only been *three* fake wolves. But you had to be there, didn't you? You wanted your bit of fun, terrorising Bo Peep's sheep!

(BEA and DEXTER step forward. Musical interlude, 'Ding Dong Bell, Pussy's in the Well' as the cast bring on big boards with 'CROOKED PIG SENSATION' and 'FREE WOLVES!' boards, which when turned round become the Courtroom furniture again. The PUBLIC and JURY reassemble. The WOLVES are back in the dock. BEA begins her TV newslink spiel.)

BEA: There were more dramatic scenes at the courtroom today, as the Wolves' trial ended after a daring escape, recapture and the discovery of sensational new evidence. The court heard how the three Pigs and Tommy Thin plotted together to turn the entire valley into one giant factory. The Wolves' lawyer made a moving plea...

(Behind BEA, the DEFENCE Lawyer, frozen, suddenly comes to confident, dramatic, table-thumping life. The PUBLIC are nodding and wiping their eyes. He's obviously moved them to tears.)

DEFENCE: The quality of mercy is not strained, ladies and gentlemen. Oh dear me, no...

PROS: *(wiping eyes)* He's right. He's right!

(EUNICE and BO PEEP are hugging. The WOLVES are grinning and giving thumbs-up signs to each other.)

DEFENCE: It must be clear to everyone that these poor Wolves have been the victims of a terrible trick, and should be released from this court forthwith, as free as Miss Peep's sheep!

KNUCK: What's forthwith?

LITTLE: *(sneering slightly)* Don't you know?

KNUCK: No.

LITTLE: It means... er... what's it mean, Big Bad?

BIG BAD: It means, let us go right now!

LITTLE: Does it? Oh, co-ol!

(The JURY have been debating quietly throughout. Now the FOREMAN turns to the JUDGE.)

FOREMAN: We say...

(A pause. Will they? Won't they?)

FOREMAN: ...Let the Wolves go free!

(The court erupts in cheers and dancing.)

JUDGE: Let them go! Let them go!

(POLICEMAN wipes his eyes and lets the WOLVES out. They dance around, shaking hands with BEA and POLLY and ALL.)

DEFENCE: And if I may say just one more thing, your Honour.

JUDGE: Of course... Anything!

SONG - PORKY PIES

(DEFENCE sings.)
Oh when you reach for that prize,
Cheating may seem an easy way,
But there is always a price to pay.

(The PIGS are being led off by the POLICEMAN.)

PIGS: *(all)* You can say that again!

(PROSECUTION sings.)
>So take a word from the wise,
>Just be fair in the things you do.

(DEFENCE sings.)
>The world will be fair right back to you.

(DEFENCE and PROSECUTION sing.)
>That's a promise, my friend.

PROS: *(speaking.)* My learned friend!

(The JUDGE comes down and joins the CLERK in a little Latin-American dance.)

(CAST sings.)
>Playing straight is the way to go,
>Try it once and before you know
>Honesty will spring up and grow
>Like a seed from the ground.

(BEA, DEXTER, POLLY and MUDDLECOMBE sing.)
>Try it once and you'll see,

(WOLVES sing.)
>It's a wonderful way to be,

(JUDGE sings.)
>And best of all it's completely free,

(CLERK sings.)
>So why not share it around!

(The JURY jump to their feet, producing maracas, and go wild. Meanwhile REST OF CAST start a dance, which develops into a conga and goes all round the hall – or the stage.)

(CAST sing)
>La la la la la – Honesty
>It's a wonderful way to be,
>La la la la la – Honesty
>Why not share it around?
>
>La la la la la la la la
>La la la la la la la la
>La la la la la la la la
>So why not share it around?

(The chorus is repeated a couple of times until NEARLY ALL THE CAST are lined up at the back. As the last voices are fading, but before the audience applauds, TOMMY is heard offstage.)

TOMMY: *(offstage)* Argh! Help!! HE-E-E-E-LP!

(TOMMY runs on, all dishevelled. The PIGS run out behind him, and pass him. The PIGS run out – preferably through the auditorium – terrified.)

TOMMY: W-W-WOLF! WOLF! WO-O-OLF!

(TOMMY THIN looks round. Everybody shrugs and ignores him. TOMMY looks into the wings. He yelps and bolts off after the PIGS. The WOLVES appear in full chase. They scramble to centre stage, yelling "Get him!" Then they see the audience and freeze for a moment.)

KNUCK: What? What?

LITTLE: Hey! We said we was innocent…

BIG BAD: We never said we was perfect!

(The WOLVES run off after TOMMY, and the CAST sing again.)

> La la la la la – Honesty,
> It's a wonderful way to be,
> La la la la la – Honesty,
> Why not share it around?
>
> Honestly!
> It's as easy as A.B.C.
> Take a handful of honesty
> And try to share it around!

THE END

Staging, Scenery and Props

Porky Pies can be staged almost anywhere – in a school hall with a stage or rostra blocks or in a classroom. If you want to go to town with sets and backdrops, please don't let me stand in your way! But most sets can be suggested by one or two simple key elements. Here are a few suggestions:

The courtroom

You will need to define five areas:
The jury box
A public gallery
The Judge's podium
The dock
Desks for the lawyers

The first two can be simple propped flats, or painted hardboard for the children to stand or sit behind. Or you could have desks, temporarily joined, and hung at the front with paper painted with representation of panelled wood.

The Judge's podium and the dock should be slightly higher than the rest of the court and behind a suggestion of wooden panels. It would be very effective to have a tallish flat as the imposing back of the Judge's throne, with a crest at the top, and a suggestion of red upholstery.

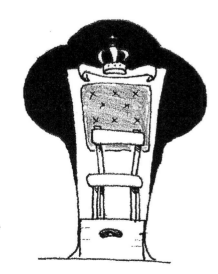

The lawyers can sit at very simple, light tables.

The countryside

This scene requires the presence of some sort of tree on either side (or simply a few branches above head height), and a tuffet. The tuffet could be a painted wooden box, or an upturned bucket with some plastic grass draped over it.

The Marys' house

The Marys have sold up, so the house is represented by one piece – a "sold" sign on a stand. Have fun thinking of a topical name for the estate agents!!

Staging, Scenery and Props

Mother Hubbard's

Mother Hubbard's shop is represented by the sales counter, preferably on castors or some form of trolley, allowing her to wheel it on and off from the wings herself. (Perhaps it could have the jury box front on the other side.)

Painted cut-out

The Pigs' House

This set doesn't actually require anything at all, but a little trio of stools or small chairs might be a nice touch. It would also be somewhere to put the model of the factory, where the audience can still see it.

Props

I have tried to keep props to a minimum, and to make sure that they can be simply produced. Set up a props table backstage so the actors can collect their own props before they go on stage.

Here are some suggestions for making your own props.

Dexter's film camera

A shoebox, with a polystyrene food tray stuck to it, a deodorant cap stuck on for a lens, the whole covered and reinforced with papier-mâché. Paint it grey and black, add a rim of corrugated cardboard to the lens, and some old bottle tops and stuff for buttons and sliders. A bit of cut-and-painted foam for a shoulder-rest, and you have the makings of an effective camera!

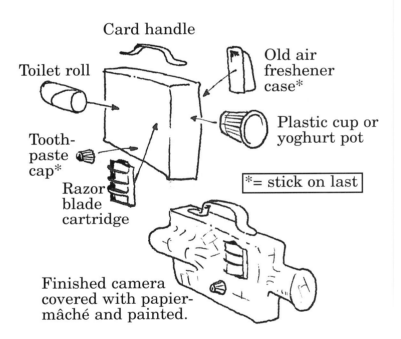

Card handle

Toilet roll

Old air freshener case*

Tooth-paste cap*

Plastic cup or yoghurt pot

Razor blade cartridge

*= stick on last

Finished camera covered with papier-mâché and painted.

Factory model

With the addition of some old water bottles and egg boxes – also covered and painted – a tray could become a very impressive 'architects model' of the Pigs' proposed factory.

Bea's lucky paper clip

This needs to be fairly distinctive and easily seen. Rather than use a small paper clip, I suggest you make one about the size of a pencil box, and make it from a length of wire coat hanger. Either leave it grey, or, for high visibility, get someone to wrap it in coloured tape!

Staging, Scenery and Props

Pig Malion's walkie-talkie and Mother Hubbard's cash register
These can all be made from cardboard boxes, covered with papier-mâché and painted.

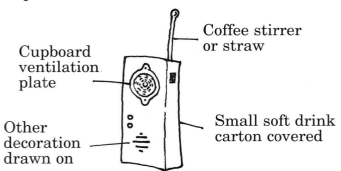

Cupboard ventilation plate

Coffee stirrer or straw

Other decoration drawn on

Small soft drink carton covered

Other props (which should be fairly easy to find or borrow) are:

Suitcases for the Mary family,
A **gavel** or small mallet for the judge
Notebooks for Bea and Muddlecombe
Papers and a document case or **briefcase** for the defence lawyer.
A **crook** for Bo Peep
A **wolf-tail** for Raglan
Maracas or shakers for the Jury at the end.

Casting and Auditions

Most of the characters have been written with very clear character traits – the Prosecution lawyer, for instance is posh, and languid, and a big-head. The Defence is bumbly and hesitant. Pig Iron is bossy; Pig Sty is sneaky. Polly Flinders is efficient and to the point, Muddlecombe slower and more considered, and so on. I hope this will enable children to latch on to their characters very quickly and really enjoy finding big broad performances for them.

There are 25 definite speaking parts, from the one line to the 'through role', which, with doubling up, can come down to 20. Little Bad Wolf is nice, as is Mr Mary, but they can be dispensed with if you have a small cast, their important lines being absorbed into other roles. The play would certainly survive the loss of a few more small parts.

It's a lot to ask of one young person to 'carry' a show like this, so I have specifically written a play with no absolute lead role. At the same time I have tried to ensure that even the small-part characters get a couple of nice lines each – preferably funny ones.

Groups

As well as spreading the casting, I have tried to created 'chorus-groups' of flexible size. There are three main chorus groups – the Jury, the Public and the Sheep. These groups can be as large or small as you need them to be, although I suggest a minimum of three children per group. There is a baying mob in the second half of the show. I'm assuming members of the Jury, Sheep and Public will play these in different costumes. However, if you have a four-form entry and a sea of children, they can be a whole new group!

Costumes and Masks

Don't panic! Obviously very few schools can run to a big costume budget. I have tried to be mindful of this, so here are a few costume suggestions. I'll deal with masks in a separate section.

Bea
Anything that makes her look like a news reporter, be it the modern, tailored look, or the old fashioned trench coat and trilby.

Dexter
Street casual – blouson jacket, T-shirt, jeans. And a baseball cap worn backwards.

Judge
A borrowed wig would be fantastic, a cotton wool fake would be great (but they do moult!) and even a wig made of rolls of white paper stuck on a base can be perfectly effective. If you can't get a red robe of any kind, then change the reference in the song to "black", and scrounge a graduation gown from someone.

Lawyers/clerk
Again, a graduation gown is great for the Prosecutor to swagger about in, or for the Defence to get tangled in. Shirts, ties, grey trousers underneath.

Policeman
Any black jacket with long sleeves. Find a few silver buttons, or cover the existing ones with foil. A few chequered bands sewn on shoulders, cuffs, breast pocket should complete the picture.

Jury/Public
The jury can wear their own clothes, though it might be fun to invite children to choose a nursery character, and design a look that suggests that person – Incey Wincey Spider? Mr & Mrs Jack Spratt? The Lion and the Unicorn? – using old clothes of their own or from a charity shop.

Wolves
As well as looking wolfish, the wolves also need to look down-at-heel. Old shoes, scruffy trousers badly gathered with belts or string. Collarless shirts, or shirts with collars that have seen their best. And jackets or waistcoats in anything vaguely 'hairy' or suggestive of forest-life – like tweed, for example, or brown corduroy. The only crucial thing is the tails, which are necessary to the plot. You can borrow one for Raglan to show, as long as your wolves have a full set for the second court scene.

Costumes and Masks

Sheep

If each child playing a sheep can find a woollen roll-neck sweater, you're half way there. Simple hooves can be made by cutting up plastic bottles and covering them with black tape, or good old papiermâché and paint. White leggings would look good – especially if they are ribbed. And black pumps!

Pigs

The Pigs should be portly. A waistcoat that is too big for the young actor, so that you can put a cushion under his shirt, would give him that 'porker' look. Malion should look younger than the others – perhaps wearing a baseball cap. The pigs should have pink tails. Make small tapered-candle shapes from pink satin. Insert some more of that copper wire and then stuff them.

Tommy Thin

The costume should be reminiscent of the Georgie Porgie figure from old books – knickerbocker suit, breeches. I see the cap as a variation of that little hat you used to see David Livingstone pictured in, with a 'curtain cord' tassel, though an old-fashioned school cap would do. Although it isn't seen till the end of the play, it should match the outfit, so that when they are put together, there is instant recognition.

Bo Peep

In my mind's eye, Bo Peep has always been a cross between a Dresden shepherdess and a *Gone with the Wind* southern belle. If you like that traditional look... scrounge an old bridesmaid's dress. Buy some cheap material of a similar colour to cover a simple bonnet shape made out of card. Attach a length of matching ribbon and with any luck you'll be well on the way to a convincing arcadian shepherdess.

Costumes and Masks

Masks

There are quite a few animals in this play. I'm sure most teachers know how to make masks anyway, but for any who missed that week at college, here are some basic tips on making a mask base, and some ideas for how to build on it:

Base

The traditional simple skull cap, consisting of a band of heavy card (supermarket fruit boxes are a good source) around the head just above brow height, plus a band across from ear to ear, and another from front to back. Staple and tape the joins, to be sure. If the mask is likely to be heavy, extend and reinforce the 'ear-to-ear' bands so that they stick out below the brow band, attach laces to these, and tie the mask under the chin for performance.

Wolf

You can make a good wolf muzzle shape out of an old plastic water bottle. Attach it firmly to the front of the base with some heavy tape (eg gaffer tape) and then cover the whole thing with papier mâché. Make holes from side to side and feed black, sheathed copper wire through them for some wonderfully ragged and twisty looking whiskers. Paint it grey, add triangular ear shapes of grey paper on the ear-to-ear band, and perhaps – if you can run to it – wire on some ping pong ball eyes.

Sheep

Follow the same principle with the sheep, but I would recommend a few extra bands to form a base for some 'fleece', made of paper, cut and curled. Cut oval shaped ears from black card. I would dispense with the nose, and simply put some face paint on each young actor to give him or her that black-faced sheep look.

Pigs

Again, the same base. This time the ears are pink triangles. The snout can be made out of yogurt pots, stuck well, covered in paper, and painted (see diagram).

Mr Big-Pig

This mask has to be slightly different as, whatever they might suspect, or guess when they see the knickerbocker costume he's wearing, the audience shouldn't know it's Tommy Thin until the mask comes off. I suggest a solidly-made papier-mâché shell formed around a balloon, with the same ears and yogurt-carton nose, but almost full-face, except for the area around the mouth. It will need to be padded with foam to fit the actor's head, and of course will need eye holes.

Song and Dance

There are seven songs in the play. Music is given for voice with guitar chords, though you might get better variety with a keyboard. If you have no musicians on the staff, there is usually an enthusiastic musical parent who can help out. The songs are written in a variety of pastiche styles, which I hope will inspire you to have fun with backing vocals and movement. *Wolf Song*, for example, is crying out for some gentle *doo-wops* in the background, and some bolero backing in the middle – especially if you decide to have some wolf friends in the public gallery.

The Only Ewe is a spoof Country and Western song, and I would love any budding Tammy Wynette out there to go for it full throttle. Meanwhile the sheep can have fun with backing *baas*. Some are written in, but feel free to expand on them.

In the final number, *Porky Pies*, which I've tried to give a slight *Begin the Beguine* feel, I hope you and the children will throw in *Oohs* and *Ahs* and *Arribas* and *Ay-ay-ays* and *Eh, Muchachos!* and anything else that makes the thing feel Latin-American. Elsewhere, please feel free to make the most of any other possibilities that present themselves. It's your show now!

Music for Songs

A Good Clean Trial

Court Will Rise

Slow, serious march ♩ = 132

1. When a crime's been com – mit – ted and it's caused a shock, And a
2. He's as brave and im – pres – sive as a Su – per – man, All the

per – son's been ar – rest – ed and they're sit – ting in the dock, When you need some – one as stea – dy as a
crooks need do is look at him and they know where they stand. Just the same chance as a snow – ball in a

1.
light – house rock, All rise for the wise old Judge.

2.
fry – ing pan! So I bid you rise,

As the case he tries, He's the wise . . . old . . . Judge!_____

I am the Judge

Wolf Song

With a lazy swing

Spoken: Your Hon - our – Mem - bers of the Ju - ry, When I see some - thing small and fur - ry, I get this rum - bly feel - ing deep in - side, And I get a sort of hunch I'm a - bout to meet my lunch It is - n't plea - sant, but it is - n't Ho - mi - cide!

Sung: Be - cause I'm a

I wish I was

Wolf_____ it don't make me a sin - ner Though it's true I'm par - tial to a bun - ny for din - ner. Hey, hey, I'm a - fraid, folks,_____ It's the way I was made, folks. I'm not a cow, I could - n't chow on grass and, Hey! May - be that's why I'm in the dock to - day!___ A sin - gle

cute_____ like a cu - tey ko - a - la, A ko - a - la they'd in - vite right in - to the par - lour, But no one e - quipped us_____ to di - gest eu - ca - lyp - tus, So I'm a car - ni - vore just like my mum and dad. That is why ev - 'ry - bo - dy says I'm bad.___ Now let's be

kind - ly word my soul I'd glad - ly sell for, But ev - 'ry time I walk on - to their land – The far - mers all rush out to greet us with the twelve - bore, They ne - ver e - ven try to un - der - stand.___

clear, I don't ap - pear wear - ing sheep's cloth - ing, I'm not a - shamed of who or what I am. But ev - 'ry - where I go I just see hate and loath - ing, And all be - cause I like a leg o' lamb!___

But then I'm a Wolf –_____ I'm a stran - ger to love, But that does - n't mean I've done the things they're ac - cus - ing me of. So please hear our cries, folks We're three in - no - cent guys, folks!___ Oh, we may be pret - ty sca - ry, An' we're far from ve - ge - ta - ri - an, But un - der - neath, we're de - cent through and through. If you knew us, you would know that's true!

The Only Ewe That I Adore

Country and western style

1. I led my flock (that's us) to play out in the mea-dow, A thing I've
2. She told her team to let off steam down in the mea-dow, I closed my
3. I put a sign on ev-'ry tree out in the mea-dow, I asked a -

done a hun-dred times be - fore._____ But lit - tle did I know that
eyes, five min - utes no - thing more,_____ I woke from sleep to find no
round I went from door to door –_____ But not one peep a - bout my

day out in the mea - dow, I'd lose the on - ly ewe that I a - dore._____
sheep out in the mea - dow, I'd lost the on - ly ewe that I a -
sheep was ev - er said – Oh! I'd lost the on - ly ewe that I a -

- dore._____ Oh I hol -lered and I whis - tled, I e - ven sang their fav - 'rite
- dore:_____ Oh I hol -lered and I whis - tled,____ and I searched both near____ and

song, I thought the on - ly crook in town was in my hand, but I was wrong.
far – And it was as the moon was ris - ing that I heard a plain - tive 'Baa'!

And pale and thin my sheep crept in to the mea- dow, So scared their wool was e - ven

whi - ter than be - fore,_____ But now I cry most ev - 'ry day . . . 'Cos there's

one still M. I. A . . . . I've lost the on - ly ewe that I a - dore . . ._____ Baaaa!

We Haven't Got a Clue

Porky Pies

Latin American cha-cha-cha ♩ = 126

Oh when you reach for that prize,
So take a word from the wise,

Cheat-ing may seem an ea-sy way,—
Just be fair in the things you do——

But there is al-ways a price to pay.—
The world will be fair right back to you.—

You can say that a - gain!
That's a pro-mise, my friend.

Play-ing straight is the way to go,—
La la la la la— Ho - nes- ty,—

Try it once and be - fore you— know—
It's a won-der-ful way to— be.—

—— Ho-nes- ty will spring up and grow—
—— La la la la la— Ho - nes- ty,—

Like a seed from the ground.
Why not share it a - round?

Try it once and you'll see,
La la la la la— Ho - nes- ty,—

It's a won-der-ful way to be.—
It's a won-der-ful way to be,—

And best of all it's com - plete - ly free,—
La la la la la Ho - nes- ty,—

So why not share it a - round!
So why not share it a - round?

Ho-nest - ly!

It's as ea-sy as A - B - C,

Take a hand-ful of

ho - nes - ty——

And try to share it a - round!————